ECHOES OF THE MIND

MITESH HOOD

Made with ♥ on the Notion Press Platform
www.notionpress.com

Contents

Preface

Dear Reader,

Within the pages of this book lies a journey unlike any other—a journey through the remarkable life of Jason. But this is no ordinary tale. Jason's story is one of mystery and imagination, of triumphs and tribulations that will captivate your mind and tug at your heartstrings.

As you delve into the depths of Jason's world, you'll be transported to a realm where reality intertwines with fantasy, where the boundaries of imagination are pushed to their limits. You'll witness the extraordinary bond between Jason and his imaginary friends, and the profound impact they have on his life.

But beneath the surface of this fantastical adventure lies a deeper truth—a truth about the resilience of the human spirit, the power of love, and the indomitable force of the human imagination. Jason's journey will leave you questioning what is real and what is imagined, and longing to uncover the secrets hidden within.

So, dear reader, prepare to be swept away on a journey of discovery and wonder. Open your mind, open your heart, and embark on an adventure that will stay with you long after you turn the final page.

Yours in curiosity,
Mitesh

Prologue

Jason's life was a magnificent tapestry woven with threads of imagination and reality. From his earliest days, he embraced the whimsical dance of his mind, guided by imaginary friends who whispered wisdom and solace in his ear. Through trials and triumphs, Jason emerged as a beacon of compassion and wisdom, his heart overflowing with love for his family.

CHAPTER ONE

A World of One

Jason Woods entered the world on a crisp autumn morning in the quaint and picturesque town of Heaven Heights. Nestled amidst rolling hills and verdant valleys, Heaven Heights was a peaceful haven, its cobblestone streets adorned with charming cottages, their facades enveloped in ivy and wisteria. Gardens burst with vibrant blooms, painting a tapestry of colours that danced in the gentle breeze. The Woods family resided in a cozy abode on Maple Street, a homely refuge where the scent of freshly baked bread often wafted from Margaret's kitchen, mingling with the fragrant aroma of Harold's morning coffee. Harold, Jason's father, was a wordsmith employed at the local newspaper, where he meticulously crafted tales of the town's events and its colourful denizens.

From the earliest moments of his existence, Jason exhibited a remarkable propensity for imagination. While his peers frolicked in the verdant parks or enthusiastically joined little league teams, Jason gravitated towards the solitude of his own backyard. There, amidst the rustling leaves and dappled sunlight, he found solace in the freedom of his wandering thoughts. Despite the unwavering love and attention bestowed upon him by his parents, they were often ensnared by the intricacies of their own lives and obligations. Harold found refuge in the sanctum of his writing, fervently penning tales that danced upon the pages of the newspaper, while Margaret devoted her days to the culinary arts and the meticulous care of their verdant garden.

Devoid of siblings or kindred spirits, Jason found himself engulfed in the embrace of solitude more often than not. Though the children of Heaven Heights extended their amiable hands in friendship, Jason's innate shyness hindered the formation of intimate bonds. The echoes of solitary play reverberated through the corridors of his consciousness, leaving him yearning for companionship. Yet, amidst the stillness of his backyard sanctuary, an extraordinary occurrence transpired, altering the course of his existence forever.

On a day when the sun cast its golden rays upon the emerald expanse of his backyard, Jason found himself engrossed in a game with his cherished toy soldiers, beneath the sprawling branches of the ancient oak tree. As his imagination soared amidst the clashing of miniature armies, a figure emerged from the depths of his subconscious, shattering the boundaries between reality and fantasy.

"Jason," the knight proclaimed, his form resplendent in gleaming armour, "I am Max, and I am here to be your friend."

Jason's eyes widened in awe and wonder, his heart quickening with exhilaration. "Are you real?" he queried, his voice trembling with anticipation.

"In a sense," Max replied, his countenance adorned with a knowing smile, "I exist as you perceive me to be."

Jason's mother, Margaret, observed her son from the kitchen window, a furrow of concern creasing her brow.

She exchanged a worried glance with Harold, who had just returned from his day at the newspaper.

"Harold, have you noticed how often Jason plays alone in the backyard?" Margaret asked, her voice tinged with worry. "I fear he's becoming too isolated."

Harold gazed out the window, watching as Jason conversed animatedly with his imaginary friend. A soft smile played across his lips as he observed the spark of creativity that ignited his son's imagination.

"He's always had a vivid imagination, Margaret," Harold replied, his tone gentle yet assured. "Perhaps this is just his way of exploring the world around him."

Margaret sighed, her concern lingering like a shadow in the recesses of her mind. "I suppose you're right, Harold. But I can't help but worry about him. He's such a sensitive boy, and I don't want him to feel lonely."

Harold placed a comforting hand on Margaret's shoulder, offering her a reassuring smile. "Jason will find his way, my dear. And we'll be here to support him every step of the way."

Meanwhile, in the backyard, Jason and Max engaged in spirited conversation, their voices carrying on the breeze like echoes of a forgotten melody.

"Do you ever wonder what lies beyond the borders of our kingdom?" Jason mused; his gaze fixed upon the distant horizon.

Max nodded thoughtfully, his armour gleaming in the soft light of dusk. "Indeed, my friend. The world is vast and filled with wonders beyond imagining. But for now, let us revel in the adventures that await us within the confines of our kingdom."

Their conversations ranged from the mundane to the fantastical, each word a testament to the enduring bond that bound them together. They spoke of their hopes and dreams, their fears, and uncertainties, sharing their innermost thoughts without reservation.

And amidst the laughter and camaraderie, there were moments of quiet reflection, when the weight of the world pressed upon their shoulders like an invisible burden. It was during these moments that their friendship shone brightest, a beacon of light amidst the encroaching darkness.

As the years passed and childhood beckoned towards adolescence, Jason and Max remained steadfast companions, their bond unbreakable and true. Though the world outside may have changed, the kingdom of their imagination remained a sanctuary of solace and adventure, a testament to the enduring power of friendship and the beauty of a world imagined. And in the heart of Jason Woods, the spirit of Max would forever roam, a timeless reminder of the magic that dwells within us all.

CHAPTER TWO

The Imaginary Companions

As Jason grew, so did his imaginary world. His adventures with Max soon felt incomplete, and thus, more characters emerged. One day, as Jason and Max were wandering through their imaginary forest, a tiny figure with sparkling wings appeared before them.

"Who are you?" Jason asked, his eyes wide with curiosity.

"I'm Amber," the fairy replied, her voice tinkling like bells. "I've come to bring a little magic to your world."

Jason grinned. "Magic? That sounds amazing!"

Amber flitted around Jason's head, sprinkling imaginary fairy dust. "With a bit of imagination, anything is possible," she said with a wink.

Finn, a wise old wizard with a long beard and a staff, was the next to join their group. He appeared one evening as Jason and Max sat by their imaginary campfire, discussing their next adventure.

"Greetings, young adventurers," Finn said, his voice deep and resonant. "I am Finn, the wizard. I have travelled far to share my wisdom with you."

Max stood up and bowed. "Welcome, Finn. We are honoured to have you join us."

These characters became his closest friends, each one embodying traits that Jason admired and aspired to. Every day after school, Jason would rush home, eager to reunite with his friends. The backyard became a stage for countless stories, each more elaborate than the last. Max taught him bravery, Amber showed him the joy of mischief, and Finn shared his ancient wisdom. Through these interactions, Jason learned valuable lessons about courage, creativity, and problem-solving.

Margaret and Harold noticed their son's vivid imagination, but they saw it as a harmless phase. They were happy that Jason had found a way to entertain himself, even if it was unconventional. Little did they know, these imaginary friends would become a permanent fixture in his life.

One evening, as the sun dipped below the horizon and the stars began to twinkle in the indigo sky, Jason sat with Max, Amber, and Finn by their imaginary campfire. The flames danced and flickered, casting long shadows across the backyard as they shared tales of their most daring exploits.

"It's moments like these that I cherish the most," Jason remarked, his voice tinged with nostalgia. "The warmth of the fire, the laughter of friends... it's like time stands still."

Max nodded, his eyes gleaming with understanding. "Indeed, Jason. These moments are precious, for they remind us of the magic that dwells within our hearts."

Amber fluttered around Jason's head, her wings shimmering in the firelight. "And the magic of friendship," she added, her voice soft yet filled with conviction. "For as long as we stand together, there is nothing we cannot overcome."

Finn gazed into the flickering flames, his expression thoughtful. "Each of us brings something unique to this group," he said, his voice heavy with wisdom. "And together, we are stronger than we could ever be alone."

As they sat together beneath the star-studded sky, a sense of belonging washed over Jason like a warm embrace. In the presence of his imaginary companions, he felt truly alive, as if the boundaries of reality had melted away, leaving only the boundless expanse of his imagination.

But amidst the laughter and camaraderie, there were moments of quiet reflection, when the weight of the world pressed upon their shoulders like an invisible burden. It was during these moments that their friendship shone brightest, a beacon of light amidst the encroaching darkness.

One afternoon, as Jason returned home from school, he found Margaret sitting in the backyard, her eyes fixed on the spot where Jason and his imaginary friends often gathered.

"Mom, what are you doing out here?" Jason asked, his curiosity piqued.

Margaret smiled, her expression filled with warmth and affection. "I was just thinking about you and your friends," she said, her voice soft yet filled with love. "You spend so much time together, I thought I'd come and join you for a while."

Jason's heart swelled with gratitude as he sat beside his mother, the familiar sights and sounds of the backyard filling him with a sense of peace and contentment. In that moment, surrounded by the love of his family and the companionship of his imaginary friends, Jason realized that he was truly blessed.

As the years passed and Jason ventured forth into the uncharted waters of adolescence, his bond with Max, Amber, and Finn remained unbreakable. They were more than just imaginary companions; they were his guiding lights, his steadfast allies, and his most cherished confidants.

And though the sands of time may have swept away the innocence of childhood, the magic of their friendship endured, a timeless testament to the power of imagination and the beauty of a world shared. For in the heart of every dreamer lies the seed of adventure, waiting to be sown amidst the fertile soil of possibility. And as long as there are stars in the sky and dreams to be dreamed, the spirit of Jason and his imaginary companions will forever roam the halls of memory, a timeless reminder of the boundless wonders that await those who dare to believe.

High school graduation marked a significant turning point in Jason's life. With his imaginary friends' guidance, he had excelled academically and earned a scholarship to a prestigious university. However, the prospect of leaving Heaven Heights and stepping into the unknown filled him with anxiety.

CHAPTER THREE

Growing Together

As the years unfolded, Jason's imaginary companions matured alongside him, evolving into more than mere figments of his imagination. Max transcended his role as a knight to become a mentor, a guiding beacon in Jason's tumultuous journey through adolescence.

"Max, I'm nervous about the math test tomorrow," Jason confided one afternoon as they sat beneath the comforting shade of the oak tree.

Max placed a reassuring hand on Jason's shoulder, his armour glinting in the dappled sunlight. "You've studied hard, Jason. Believe in yourself. Face the challenge head-on, just like you would a dragon."

With Max's encouragement, Jason faced his fears with renewed determination, finding solace in the wisdom of his stalwart friend.

Amber, once a playful sprite, blossomed into a confidante, her understanding heart attuned to Jason's deepest fears and insecurities. One evening, as Jason sat on his bed, feeling the weight of the world pressing down upon him, he turned to Amber for comfort.

"Amber," he whispered, his voice tinged with vulnerability, "sometimes I feel like I don't fit in."

Amber fluttered beside him, her delicate wings shimmering in the moonlight. "It's okay to feel that way, Jason," she said, her voice soft and soothing. "Remember, you are unique, and that's what makes you special. Never lose your sense of wonder."

With Amber's gentle words echoing in his heart, Jason found solace in the knowledge that he was not alone in his struggles.

Finn, the wise old wizard, deepened in wisdom with each passing year, his advice offering profound insights into the complexities of life. During a particularly tumultuous time, when Jason was grappling with the daunting task of choosing his future path, he sought Finn's sage counsel.

"Finn, how do I know what's right for me?" Jason asked, his brow furrowed in thought.

Finn stroked his beard thoughtfully, his eyes twinkling with ancient wisdom. "The right path is the one that feels true to your heart, Jason," he said, his voice resonating with quiet authority. "Trust your instincts and follow your passions. They will lead you to where you need to be."

In the halls of academia, Jason excelled, his intellect and creativity earning him the admiration of his teachers. Yet, despite his academic prowess, he remained a solitary figure, detached from the vibrant tapestry of teenage camaraderie. While his peers revelled in the joys of youth, Jason sought solace beneath the branches of the old oak tree, engaging in conversations with friends only he could see.

His detachment from real-world social interactions concerned his parents, who watched with furrowed brows as their son retreated further into the recesses of his imagination. Yet, whenever they voiced their concerns, Jason reassured them with a smile, insisting that he was happy in his own world.

As adolescence unfurled its turbulent wings, Jason encountered a myriad of challenges—peer pressure, identity crises, and academic stress—each one testing the limits of his resilience. But unlike his peers, who sought solace in the company of friends or the comforting embrace of family, Jason turned to Max, Amber, and Finn for guidance.

When a bully targeted him at school, it was Max who taught him to stand up for himself, his unwavering courage serving as a beacon of strength in the face of adversity.

"Don't let them push you around, Jason," Max advised, his voice firm and resolute. "Stand tall and show them you're not afraid."

And when self-doubt threatened to overwhelm him, Amber's playful encouragement lifted his spirits, infusing him with the confidence to confront his fears head-on.

"You're capable of amazing things, Jason. Don't ever forget that" she would say, her eyes sparkling with unwavering belief in his abilities.

But perhaps it was Finn, the venerable wizard, who offered Jason the greatest gift of all—the gift of perspective. In moments of uncertainty and doubt, it was Finn's wisdom that steadied Jason's trembling heart, guiding him towards the path of self-discovery and self-acceptance.

"Life is a series of choices, Jason. Each one shapes your destiny," Finn would counsel, his voice a soothing balm to Jason's troubled soul. "Choose wisely, and always stay true to yourself."

And so, as the years stretched out before him like an endless tapestry, Jason found solace in the enduring companionship of Max, Amber, and Finn. Together, they weathered the storms of adolescence, their bond growing stronger with each passing day.

For in the heart of every dreamer lies the seed of resilience, waiting to be nurtured amidst the fertile soil of imagination. And as long as there are stars in the sky and dreams to be dreamed, the spirit of Jason and his imaginary companions will forever roam the halls of memory, a testament to the enduring power of friendship and the beauty of a world shared.

CHAPTER FOUR

Choices and Paths

High school graduation marked a significant turning point in Jason's life. With his imaginary friends' guidance, he had excelled academically and earned a scholarship to a prestigious university. However, the prospect of leaving Heaven Heights and stepping into the unknown filled him with a mix of excitement and anxiety.

On the eve of his departure, Jason found solace under the old oak tree, the moon casting dappled shadows across the grass. Max, Amber, and Finn appeared before him; their forms illuminated by the soft glow of fireflies.

Max, his armour gleaming in the moonlight, placed a reassuring hand on Jason's shoulder. "This is your quest, Jason," he said, his voice steady and unwavering. "Embrace it with courage and determination."

Jason nodded, a knot of uncertainty tightening in his chest. "But what if I'm not ready?" he asked, his voice barely above a whisper.

Amber fluttered around him, her wings shimmering with iridescent light. "Don't forget to have fun along the way," she chimed in, her laughter like the tinkling of wind chimes. "Life is an adventure, Jason. Embrace every moment, even the ones that scare you."

Finn, his eyes twinkling with ancient wisdom, stepped forward. "Knowledge is your greatest ally, Jason," he said, his voice a soothing melody. "Seek it, and you will find your way."

With his friends' words echoing in his mind, Jason set off for university, his heart heavy with anticipation. As he stepped onto campus for the first time, he felt a surge of excitement mingled with trepidation. The campus buzzed with activity, students laughing and chatting as they hurried to their classes.

Jason's academic prowess shone as he immersed himself in his studies. His love for literature blossomed into a passion for writing, fuelled by the boundless imagination of his childhood companions. Max, Amber, and Finn remained by his side, their guidance guiding him through the complexities of academia.

But despite his success, Jason struggled to form real friendships. His roommates found him peculiar, always talking to himself or lost in thought. One evening, as Jason sat at his desk, surrounded by stacks of books and papers, his roommate Jake confronted him.

"Jason, why are you always talking to yourself?" Jake asked, his brow furrowed in confusion.

Jason hesitated, unsure how to explain. "I'm not talking to myself," he finally said, his cheeks flushing with embarrassment. "I'm talking to my friends."

Jake raised an eyebrow. "Friends? What friends?"

Jason swallowed hard, the weight of his secret pressing down on him. "They're...imaginary," he admitted, his voice barely above a whisper. "They've been with me since I was a kid."

Jake stared at him for a moment, then shrugged. "Well, as long as it works for you, man. Just don't expect everyone to understand."

Relieved that Jake hadn't mocked him, Jason smiled gratefully. But deep down, he knew that his secret would always set him apart from his peers.

As the years passed, Jason threw himself into his studies, seeking refuge in the world of academia. He spent long hours in the campus library, surrounded by books, his imaginary friends by his side. Together, they discussed his coursework, brainstorming ideas and refining his writing.

"What do you think of this story idea, Max?" Jason asked one afternoon, his pen scratching across the pages of his journal.

Max nodded thoughtfully; his brow furrowed in concentration. "It has potential, Jason," he said, his voice filled with encouragement. "Just remember to make your hero brave and true."

Amber chimed in, her eyes sparkling with excitement. "And don't forget to add a bit of magic and wonder! Every good story needs a touch of enchantment."

Finn, ever the sage, added his own insights. "A good story should also teach a lesson, Jason," he said, his voice calm and reassuring. "Something that resonates with the heart."

Their counsel never led him astray, and Jason graduated with honours, ready to face the next chapter of his life. But as he stood on the threshold of adulthood, he couldn't shake the feeling of uncertainty that lingered in the depths of his soul.

CHAPTER FIVE

An Aloof Adult

Jason's transition into adulthood was marked by professional success and personal isolation. He secured a job as an editor at a renowned publishing house, where his keen eye for detail and imaginative mind earned him rapid promotions. His colleagues respected him but found his solitary nature perplexing. Jason preferred the quiet of his office to social gatherings, his mind always half-occupied by his imaginary friends.

Despite his detachment from the social world, Jason's life was fulfilling. He lived in a charming apartment filled with books and mementos of his adventures, both real and imagined. Max, Amber, and Finn remained by his side, their presence a comforting constant in an ever-changing world. They discussed his work, helped him navigate office politics, and provided solace during moments of doubt.

One evening, as Jason sat at his desk reviewing manuscripts, Max spoke up. "This one has potential, Jason. The protagonist's journey is compelling."

Amber added, "But it needs a touch of magic. Maybe a hidden realm or a mystical artifact."

Finn nodded in agreement. "And a moral lesson, something that speaks to the reader's heart."

Jason smiled, jotting down their suggestions. "Thanks, guys. I don't know what I'd do without you."

His parents, though proud of his achievements, worried about his isolation. They encouraged him to socialize more, to find a partner, and to build a family. Jason nodded and promised to try, but his heart was tethered to the world he had created.

As Jason delved deeper into his work, the lines between reality and imagination began to blur. Max, Amber, and Finn became more than just figments of his imagination; they were his confidants, his advisors, his friends. He found himself turning to them for guidance in every aspect of his life, relying on their wisdom to navigate the complexities of adulthood.

But as the years passed, Jason's isolation grew more pronounced. His colleagues viewed him with a mixture of admiration and suspicion, unable to comprehend his obsession with his imaginary friends. They whispered behind his back, speculating about his mental state and questioning his sanity.

One afternoon, as Jason sat alone in his office, poring over manuscripts, he overheard two coworkers discussing him in hushed tones.

"Have you noticed how Jason always talks to himself?" one of them said, her voice tinged with concern.

The other shook his head. "It's not just that. He's always so...detached. Like he's living in a world of his own."

Jason's heart sank as he listened to their words. He knew that he was different, that his bond with Max, Amber, and Finn set him apart from his peers. But he couldn't bring himself to let them go; they were his lifeline, his connection to a world that existed beyond the confines of his office walls.

Despite his parents' urgings, Jason remained resolute in his solitude. He tried to socialize, to forge connections with his coworkers, but he always felt like an outsider, a stranger in a strange land. He longed for companionship, for someone who understood him, but he couldn't shake the feeling that he was destined to walk this path alone.

As the years rolled by, Jason threw himself into his work, pouring his heart and soul into every project. Max, Amber, and Finn were his constant companions, guiding him through the highs and lows of his career. They celebrated his successes and comforted him in his failures, their unwavering support a beacon of light in the darkness.

But despite their presence, Jason couldn't shake the feeling of emptiness that gnawed at his soul. He longed for something more, something real, but he didn't know how to find it. And so, he retreated further into his imaginary world, seeking solace in the familiar embrace of his friends.

One evening, as Jason sat alone in his apartment, surrounded by the trappings of his success, he felt a pang of longing pierce his heart. He longed for a family, for someone to share his life with, but he didn't know if he was capable of opening himself up to another person. He had grown so accustomed to his solitude, so comfortable in his isolation, that the thought of letting someone else in filled him with a sense of dread.

But deep down, beneath the layers of fear and uncertainty, Jason knew that he couldn't continue living like this forever. He knew that he needed to take a leap of faith, to step out of his comfort zone and embrace the unknown. And so, with a determined glint in his eye, he made a promise to himself: he would find a way to break free from the chains of his isolation, to find the courage to live his life on his own terms.

CHAPTER SIX

Love and Isolation

In his late twenties, fate introduced Jason to Cynthia. She was a colleague, new to the publishing house, with a warm smile and a genuine interest in Jason's work. Unlike others, Cynthia wasn't put off by Jason's aloofness. She admired his intelligence and was intrigued by his mysterious nature.

Their relationship blossomed slowly, like a delicate flower unfurling its petals to the warmth of the sun. Cynthia's patience and kindness gradually broke through Jason's defences, melting the icy barriers he had erected around his heart. She accepted his quirks and appreciated his uniqueness, embracing him for who he was, imaginary friends and all.

For the first time in his life, Jason felt a connection to someone outside his imaginary world. Cynthia's presence filled him with a sense of warmth and belonging that he had never known before. As they spent more time together, sharing their hopes and dreams, fears and insecurities, Jason realized that he had found his soulmate.

They married in a small ceremony, with only close family and friends present. As Jason stood at the altar, his heart pounding with excitement and nerves, he stole a glance at Cynthia, her eyes sparkling with love and anticipation. In that moment, he knew that he had found the missing piece of his puzzle, the one who would stand by his side through thick and thin.

"Jason, I love you just the way you are," Cynthia whispered one night as they lay in bed, her hand resting on his chest.

Jason looked into her eyes, feeling a warmth spread through his chest like a flickering flame. "Thank you, Cynthia," he said softly, his voice tinged with emotion. "You've brought so much light into my life."

Marriage brought new challenges, as it often does. Cynthia loved Jason deeply, but she often felt second to his imaginary friends. Jason tried to balance his dual worlds, but it was difficult. He would spend hours talking to Max, Amber, and Finn, seeking their counsel and companionship, leaving Cynthia feeling isolated and alone.

Despite this, their love endured. They had two children, Hannah, and Jack, who brought immense joy to their lives. Jason adored his children, doting on them with all the love and affection he could muster. But even as he revelled in their laughter and embraced their innocence, he couldn't shake the feeling of guilt that gnawed at his conscience.

"Daddy, who are you talking to?" Hannah asked one afternoon, finding Jason deep in conversation with Max.

Jason smiled, lifting her onto his lap and wrapping her in a warm embrace. "Just some old friends, sweetheart," he replied, brushing a stray lock of hair from her forehead.

Hannah's eyes widened with curiosity. "Can I meet them?"

Jason hesitated, unsure how to explain. "Maybe someday, Hannah," he said softly, his heart heavy with regret. "They're very special to me."

As the years passed, Jason tried to find a balance between his family and his imaginary friends, but it was a delicate dance fraught with uncertainty. He loved Cynthia and his children more than anything in the world, but he couldn't deny the pull of his imaginary world, the comfort and solace it offered in times of need.

And so, he continued to walk the tightrope between reality and fantasy, clinging to the threads of his imagination even as he reached out to embrace the tangible world before him. And through it all, Cynthia stood by his side, her love a beacon of light in the darkness, guiding him through the stormy seas of life.

CHAPTER SEVEN

Slipping Memory

As Jason entered his forties, subtle changes in his memory began to surface like ripples on a calm pond, gradually growing more pronounced with each passing day. At first, they were minor forgetting where he had left his keys or missing a meeting. Cynthia noticed these lapses but attributed them to stress and the natural process of aging. However, the incidents became more frequent and severe, casting a shadow of uncertainty over their once serene lives.

One evening, as they prepared for bed, Cynthia gently broached the subject that had been weighing heavily on her heart. "Jason, I'm worried about you. You've been forgetting things a lot lately."

Jason furrowed his brow, struggling to grasp onto the threads of memory that seemed to slip through his fingers like grains of sand. "It's just stress, Cynthia. Work has been hectic."

But Cynthia could see the fear lurking behind his words, the uncertainty that clouded his eyes like a storm on the horizon. Taking his hand in hers, she met his gaze with unwavering determination. "I think it might be more than that. Maybe we should see a doctor."

Jason sighed, feeling the weight of her concern pressing down on him like a leaden blanket. "Alright. I'll make an appointment."

The visit to the specialist was a nerve-wracking experience for Jason and his family. They sat in the sterile waiting room, the air heavy with anticipation and anxiety, until finally, they were called into the doctor's office.

Dr. Stevens, a middle-aged man with a kind smile and gentle demeanour, greeted them warmly as they entered the room. He listened attentively as Cynthia recounted Jason's symptoms, her voice trembling with worry.

After a thorough examination and a series of tests, Dr. Stevens delivered the diagnosis with a compassion that belied the gravity of the situation. "Mr. and Mrs. Thompson, I'm afraid the results are concerning. Jason is showing signs of early-onset dementia, likely exacerbated by his history of schizophrenia."

The words hung heavy in the air, a palpable weight that pressed down on Jason's chest like a suffocating embrace. He felt as though the ground had been ripped out from beneath him, leaving him adrift in a sea of uncertainty and despair.

Cynthia's eyes brimmed with tears as she reached out to clasp Jason's hand in hers, her touch a lifeline in the stormy sea of emotions that threatened to overwhelm them. "What does this mean, doctor?" she asked, her voice trembling with fear.

Dr. Stevens sighed, his expression sympathetic. "It means that Jason's condition will likely continue to deteriorate over time. We can explore treatment options to slow the progression of the disease, but unfortunately, there is no cure."

Jason felt a surge of panic rise within him, threatening to consume him whole. He had always prided himself on his intellect and his ability to navigate the complexities of life with ease. But now, faced with the prospect of losing his mind, he felt powerless, adrift in a sea of uncertainty.

Cynthia wrapped her arms around him, holding him close as tears streamed down her cheeks. "We'll get through this together, Jason," she whispered, her voice a soothing balm to his wounded soul.

And though the road ahead was fraught with uncertainty, they faced it together, hand in hand, their love a beacon of light in the darkness.

CHAPTER EIGHT

Battling the Inner Storm

Jason sat in his favourite armchair; his mind clouded by a storm of emotions. The weight of the diagnosis hung over him like a heavy shroud, suffocating him with its relentless gravity. Cynthia's presence nearby offered some solace, her hand resting gently on his shoulder, but it was a fragile comfort against the tempest raging within him.

"Daddy, what's wrong?" Hannah's voice broke through the silence, her concern palpable.

Jason looked up, forcing a smile onto his face as he tried to shield his children from his inner turmoil. "I'm okay, sweetheart," he replied, his voice strained. "Just a bit tired, that's all."

But Hannah wasn't convinced, her eyes searching his face for signs of the truth. "You don't look okay, Daddy," she insisted, her voice tinged with worry.

Jason's heart clenched at the sight of his daughter's concern, a wave of guilt washing over him like a tidal wave. "I'm sorry, Hannah," he murmured, his voice thick with emotion. "I'm just going through a tough time right now, but I'll be alright."

Jack, ever perceptive, stepped forward, his expression a mirror of his father's pain. "It's okay to be sad, Dad," he said softly, his voice filled with compassion. "We're here for you."

Tears welled up in Jason's eyes as he looked at his children, overwhelmed by their unwavering love and support. "Thank you, kids," he whispered, his voice trembling with emotion. "You have no idea how much that means to me."

Cynthia joined them, her eyes filled with empathy as she wrapped her arms around her family. "We're in this together, Jason," she said, her voice steady despite the tears in her eyes. "No matter what happens, we'll face it as a family."

And in that moment, as they held each other close, Jason felt a flicker of hope ignite within him—a small beacon of light in the darkness, guiding him through the storm that raged within.

But even as he clung to that glimmer of hope, a tide of despair threatened to pull him under. The weight of his diagnosis bore down on him like a leaden weight, crushing him beneath its relentless weight. He felt as though he were drowning, lost in a sea of uncertainty and fear.

His mind was a whirlwind of conflicting emotions—sadness, anger, fear, and despair—all swirling together in a tumultuous cacophony that threatened to consume him whole. He wanted to lash out, to scream and rage against the unfairness of it all, but he felt powerless, adrift in a sea of hopelessness.

Amidst the chaos of his own mind, the voices of his imaginary friends echoed like distant whispers, their presence a bittersweet reminder of happier times. But even they seemed to mock him now, their words a cruel reminder of all that he had lost.

"Jason, we're here for you," Max said, his voice filled with concern.

"We'll help you through this, Jason," Amber added, her wings fluttering nervously. "You're not alone."

But Jason pushed them away, his frustration mounting with each passing moment. "You're not real," he snapped, his voice laced with bitterness. "You're just figments of my imagination—a cruel trick of my mind."

Max and Amber exchanged worried glances; their faces etched with sorrow. "Jason, please," Max pleaded, his voice cracking with emotion. "We only wanted to help."

But Jason was beyond reasoning, his mind clouded by anger and resentment. He turned away from them, his heart heavy with regret, as the darkness closed in around him like a suffocating blanket.

In the days that followed, Jason's emotions continued to ebb and flow like the tide, his mind a tempest of conflicting thoughts and feelings. He would alternate between moments of profound sadness, when the weight of his diagnosis threatened to crush him beneath its crushing weight, and flashes of seething anger, directed both inward and outward.

At times, he would find himself consumed by a sense of helplessness, his mind a whirlwind of doubt and despair. "What's the point?" he would mutter to himself, his voice hollow with resignation. "There's no escaping this."

But amidst the turmoil and chaos, there were brief moments of clarity—glimpses of light in the darkness that offered a glimmer of hope amidst the despair. Cynthia's unwavering love and support remained a constant source of strength, her gentle encouragement a beacon guiding him through the storm.

"We'll get through this together, Jason," she would say, her voice filled with determination. "No matter what happens, I'll always be by your side."

And though Jason's journey was fraught with uncertainty and fear, he clung to her words like a lifeline, knowing that as long as he had her love, he could weather any storm.

But as the days turned into weeks, Jason realized that if he wanted to truly live life for his family, he needed to let go of the imaginary friends that had been his companions for so long. It was a painful realization, but one he knew was necessary for his own healing.

CHAPTER NINE

A Farewell to Friends

Determined to embrace his new reality and live fully for his family, Jason knew he needed to make a difficult decision. He sought solace under the comforting shade of the old oak tree, where countless conversations with Max, Amber, and Finn had unfolded over the years.

"Max, Amber, Finn," Jason began, his voice quivering with emotion, "I have to say goodbye."

Max stepped forward; his expression solemn yet understanding. "Why, Jason? We've always been here for you."

Jason nodded, tears welling up in his eyes. "I know, Max. And I'm grateful for everything you've done for me. But I need to focus on my real family now. They need me more than ever."

Amber's eyes shimmered with unshed tears, her voice filled with warmth and understanding. "We understand, Jason. We'll always be a part of you, no matter where life takes you."

Finn placed a reassuring hand on Jason's shoulder, his gaze filled with empathy. "Your journey with us may be ending, but your new adventure with your family is just beginning. Embrace it, Jason, and cherish every moment."

With a heavy heart, Jason thanked his imaginary friends for their unwavering support, for being his constant companions through the ups and downs of life. As they began to fade from his mind, a bittersweet mixture of sorrow and liberation washed over him.

Watching them slowly disappear, Jason felt a profound sense of loss but also a newfound freedom. He turned his attention to Cynthia, Hannah, and Jack, determined to make the most of the time he had left.

"Thank you," he whispered to the fading figures of Max, Amber, and Finn, his voice filled with gratitude and love. "I'll never forget you."

As the last traces of his imaginary friends disappeared, Jason felt a weight lift from his shoulders. He turned to his real family, his heart overflowing with love and determination.

"Let's make the most of every moment," he said to Cynthia, his voice strong despite the tears in his eyes. "Together, we can face whatever challenges come our way."

Cynthia nodded, her eyes shining with pride and love. "We're in this together, Jason. Always."

Hannah and Jack rushed into their father's arms, their laughter mingling with tears. "We love you, Daddy," they chorused, their voices filled with warmth and affection.

Jason held them close, feeling a sense of peace wash over him. Despite the challenges that lay ahead, he knew that as long as he had his family by his side, he could weather any storm.

And so, hand in hand with Cynthia, Hannah, and Jack, Jason faced the future with courage and determination, ready to embrace whatever adventures life had in store. For in the end, it was not the imaginary friends that defined him, but the love and strength of his real family that would carry him through.

CHAPTER TEN

Embracing Reality

With Max, Amber, and Finn now mere echoes of memories, Jason redirected his focus towards nurturing a deeper connection with his family. He devoted his days to cultivating precious moments with Hannah and Jack, immersing himself in their laughter, their innocence, and their boundless energy. Each interaction became a cherished memory, etched into the fabric of his being.

"Daddy, can you tell us a story?" Jack's voice filled the room one evening as they gathered in the cozy living room, the soft glow of the fireplace casting dancing shadows on the walls.

Jason's heart swelled with affection as he pulled his children close, their eager faces shining in the firelight. "Of course, my darlings," he replied, his voice filled with warmth. "Once upon a time, there was a brave knight named Max, a mischievous fairy named Amber, and a wise wizard named Finn..."

As he wove tales of his imaginary friends, Jason felt a sense of peace wash over him. Though they were no longer a tangible presence in his life, their lessons lived on in the stories he shared with his children—lessons of courage, creativity, and wisdom that would shape their hearts and minds for years to come.

But even as Jason immersed himself in the joys of fatherhood, he couldn't shake the spectre of his declining health. With each passing day, his memory continued to deteriorate, eroding the foundation of his reality. Yet, in the face of this cruel fate, Jason remained steadfast in his determination to ensure his family's future.

He meticulously organized his finances, wrote a detailed will, and prepared instructions for Cynthia to follow when he could no longer help. These practical preparations offered him a semblance of control amidst the chaos of his mind, allowing him to find solace in the knowledge that his family would be cared for long after he was gone.

But amidst the practicalities of planning for the future, Jason never lost sight of the present moment. He seized every opportunity to create lasting memories with Cynthia, savouring each tender moment shared between them.

"Cynthia," Jason said one evening as they sat on the porch, the vibrant hues of the sunset painting the sky in shades of gold and crimson, "thank you for everything. You've given me a wonderful life."

Cynthia's eyes glistened with unshed tears as she reached for Jason's hand, her touch a soothing balm to his troubled soul. "And you've given me so much more, Jason," she whispered, her voice filled with love and gratitude. "You've given me a lifetime of memories, of laughter, and of love. That's more than I could ever ask for."

In that moment, as they watched the sun dip below the horizon, casting the world in a warm embrace of twilight, Jason felt a profound sense of gratitude wash over him. Despite the challenges that lay ahead, he knew that he was blessed to have Cynthia by his side, a beacon of light guiding him through the darkest of nights.

And so, hand in hand with Cynthia, Jason embraced the reality of his situation, finding strength in the love that surrounded him and solace in the knowledge that no matter what tomorrow may bring, he would face it with courage and grace. For in the end, it wasn't the memories of his imaginary friends that defined him, but the love and devotion he shared with his family that would endure for eternity.

CHAPTER ELEVEN

The Final Years

As Jason journeyed into his fifties, the relentless march of time had taken its toll on his once-sharp mind. His memory, once a treasure trove of knowledge and experiences, now betrayed him with alarming frequency. Simple tasks became arduous challenges, and familiar places became mazes of confusion. Yet, amidst the fog of forgetfulness, Jason's spirit remained undaunted, buoyed by the unwavering love and support of his family.

"Dad, let's go for a walk," Hannah suggested one afternoon, her voice filled with warmth as she took Jason's hand in hers.

Jason smiled, his heart swelling with gratitude for his daughter's unwavering companionship. "That sounds lovely, Hannah. Lead the way."

Together, they strolled through the tranquil streets of their neighbourhood, the gentle breeze carrying whispers of memories past. With each step, Jason felt a sense of peace wash over him, grateful for the fleeting moments of clarity amidst the fog of his mind.

As the years passed, Jason's condition continued to deteriorate, his once-vibrant spirit dimmed by the relentless onslaught of his illness. Yet, even in the face of such adversity, he remained resolute in his determination to live fully—to seize every precious moment with unwavering gratitude and grace.

He recorded messages for his beloved children, pouring his heart and soul into each word, imparting wisdom, and sharing his hopes and dreams for their future. He wrote letters to Cynthia, expressing his undying love and gratitude for the unwavering support she had shown him throughout their journey together. These acts of foresight, though tinged with sadness, served as a testament to the depth of his love and the resilience of his spirit.

As Jason's condition progressed, there came a heartbreaking moment when he struggled to recognize even the faces of his beloved children. Confusion clouded his eyes as he gazed at Hannah and Jack, unable to place their familiar features.

"Who are they?" Jason asked, his voice tinged with a hint of desperation, turning to Cynthia for reassurance.

Cynthia's heart shattered at the realization of her husband's struggle. With tears glistening in her eyes, she whispered softly, "They're our children, Jason. They're Hannah and Jack."

A flicker of recognition crossed Jason's face as he turned back to his children, his expression softening with a mixture of content and joy. Despite the fog of his mind, the love he held for them remained a steadfast beacon in the darkness.

With a gentle smile, he reached out to them, his eyes filled with an overwhelming sense of love and gratitude. Though his memories may fade, the bond he shared with his family transcended the boundaries of time and space, a testament to the enduring power of love.

As Jason neared the end of his journey, his family gathered around him, their love a comforting embrace in his final moments. Cynthia clasped his hand tightly, her eyes brimming with tears as she whispered words of love and solace. "I'm here, Jason," she murmured, her voice trembling with emotion. "I'll always be here."

Jason turned to her, his gaze filled with a mixture of love and gratitude. "Thank you, Cynthia," he whispered, his voice barely a whisper. "For everything."

Hannah and Jack stood by his bedside; their faces etched with sorrow as they clung to each other for support. "We love you, Dad," they chorused, their voices trembling with emotion.

Jason reached out to them, his touch a gentle caress against their tear-streaked cheeks. "Remember," he said softly, his voice filled with a quiet strength. "Life is precious. Treasure every moment, for you never know when it may slip away."

His words hung heavy in the air, a poignant reminder of the fleeting nature of existence. And as his loved ones held him close, Jason felt a sense of peace wash over him, knowing that his legacy would endure—a legacy of love, of courage, and of unwavering determination in the face of adversity.

With one last smile, Jason closed his eyes, his heart overflowing with love as he embraced the eternal embrace of sleep. His spirit soared on wings of love, carried forth into the boundless expanse of eternity, leaving behind a legacy of love that would endure for generations to come.

CHAPTER TWELVE

A Legacy of Love

Jason's life was a magnificent tapestry woven with threads of imagination and reality. From his earliest days, he embraced the whimsical dance of his mind, guided by imaginary friends who whispered wisdom and solace in his ear. Through trials and triumphs, Jason emerged as a beacon of compassion and wisdom, his heart overflowing with love for his family.

As Jason's family gathered to reminisce, the memories of his vibrant spirit filled the room, painting the walls with hues of laughter and warmth. Cynthia, Hannah, and Jack leafed through old photo albums, each image a snapshot of a life well lived—a life interwoven with love and adventure.

"Your father was a remarkable man," Cynthia said, her voice soft with emotion as she gazed at the faded photographs. "He taught us all so much about courage and love."

Hannah smiled through tears, her fingers tracing the outline of her father's face in a cherished photograph. "I miss him," she confessed, her voice quivering with emotion.

Jack wrapped his arm around his sister, offering her silent comfort as they shared their grief. "Me too," he whispered, his own eyes shimmering with unshed tears.

"But we have each other, and we have Dad's memories."

Cynthia's heart swelled with love for her children, grateful for the bond that held them together through life's trials. "Yes," she agreed, her voice trembling with emotion. "We'll always have his love to guide us."

As the years passed, Cynthia watched her children blossom into remarkable individuals, their lives a testament to Jason's enduring legacy. Hannah pursued her passion for literature, her words weaving tales of love and adventure that echoed her father's spirit. Meanwhile, Jack became a dedicated teacher, inspiring young minds with his passion for learning and kindness.

Through it all, Cynthia remained a pillar of strength, her love for Jason burning bright in her heart. Though the years had etched lines on her face and silvered her hair, her spirit remained undaunted, fuelled by the love she shared with her family.

In the quiet moments that followed, as they sat together in the warmth of their home, surrounded by memories of their beloved husband and father, Cynthia, Hannah, and Jack felt a deep sense of peace. Though Jason was no longer with them in body, his spirit lived on in their hearts, a guiding light in times of darkness.

And as they looked to the future, filled with both uncertainty and promise, they knew that Jason would be with them every step of the way. For his legacy was not measured in years, but in the love, he shared and the lives he touched—a legacy that would endure for generations to come.